The Treasure of Misty Glen

By Jane Claire Lambert

Pulished in Kansas City by Jane Claire Lambert.
Publisher's Note: This novel is a work of fiction. Names, characters, places, and incidents are either products of the author's imagination or used fictitiously. All charactors are fictional and any similarity to people living or dead is purely coincidental.

Library of Congress
Cataloging-in-Publication Data
Lambert, Jane Claire
The Treasure of Misty Glen
ISBN 978-1-888659-20-7

Printed in the United States of America

This book is lovingly dedicated to:
Amanda, our friend, who got the ball rolling
and Lily, our grandgirl, who kept it all going

The Treasure of Misty Glen

CHAPTER ONE

The Letter

The pale blue envelope was addressed to Mr. and Mrs. Zachary Bigelow, Detroit. Postmarked from a tiny town near the snow belt of Michigan, it was written in the careful flowing script of a time long ago.

After Mr. and Mrs. Bigelow had each read the enclosed letter twice, they spoke together quietly for several minutes.

Their conversation was punctuated with laughter and interrupted more than once as they reread a sentence or two from the beautifully penned letter to make sure they understood the details. At last, they called their two oldest children into the living room.

As soon as Tim and Sophie were seated, their father began, "You remember my friend, Jeremy? We've just received an interesting letter from Jeremy's aunt, Jenny MacNeil. I know you've heard us speak of her, though you've never met."

They nodded as their father continued. "Mrs. MacNeil lives on a farm three hours northwest of here. She's doing well and has plenty of help with the heavy farm work, but she says she's rather lonely."

Tim and Sophie exchanged confused glances with one another as they wondered what all of this had to do with them.

"She wrote," said Mother, "to ask if you both would like to come and stay with her for two weeks during your winter holidays. She doesn't expect you to spend all your time with her; she'd just like to have some young ones around the house to 'do for,' as she puts it.

"Your father and I have discussed it. We think you're old enough and you'd be welcome to go if you wished. So, think it over and let us know how we should reply to her invitation."

Tim and Sophie slowly turned and stared at each other. Take a trip? For two whole weeks? To stay at a farm way out in the country?

Little by little, a grin spread over Tim's face and was reflected in his sister's soft brown eyes.

"Sounds like it could be an adventure in the making."

"Yes!" Sophie whispered.

"Mom! Dad! We'd love to go to the country and stay with Mrs. MacNeil, if it's really all right with you!"

CHAPTER TWO

Armchair Inquiry

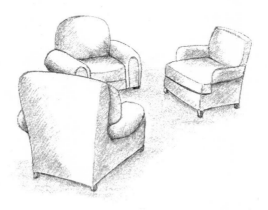

As soon as the initial wave of excitement passed, Tim and his sister grew curious and captured their father by corralling him with their armchairs. Then they began firing their questions.

"What sort of farm and what kinds of animals?" asked Sophie.

"How old is Mrs. MacNeil?" Tim wanted to know.

"Was there a Mr. MacNeil? If so, what happened to him?" queried Sophie softly.

"Have you ever been to her farm? Who helps her if we don't have to do the heavy work?" wondered Tim.

"Whoa!" laughed the children's father, throwing up his hands to cover his face, "I'm not sure I can remember that many questions."

Settling back in his chair, he thought for a moment. "Let me see, Jeremy's Aunt Jenny must be about sixty years old. She did marry, but she didn't have children of her own. Her husband, John, was a farmer.

"He loved the country. Made a good living at farming, and she worked right alongside him and loved it, too. Five years ago he died from complications of pneumonia. After that,

Mrs. MacNeil was determined to keep the farm and run it as her husband had done for so many years.

"It's true that she's had to scale down a few of their farm projects, but she still grows squash and some sugar beets for market, and of course, corn, just like they always did."

"What on earth is a sugar beet?" Tim wanted to know.

Father grinned, "A sugar beet is a root vegetable that has sugar in it. Sugar beets are used to make some of our white table sugar, and I think more of 'em come from our state than any other.

"However, the ones from the MacNeil farm don't become table sugar; they're used instead for cattle and deer feed."

Finding himself at the end of his sugar beet expertise, the

children's father tried to remember the rest of the questions. "Let's see now, I'm not really sure who is helping her with all the work, but I bet you'll find out," he said, smiling, "and… what else?"

"The animals!" cried Sophie excitedly.

Father laughed, "Of course—the animals. Well, I know they had a horse. It was a dapple-gray Percheron—raised it from a baby—and there's probably a dog. I bet she has a cow for milk and a few chickens for eggs, but I don't know about other animals, because the farm was mostly cash crops. Okay?" he grinned at Sophie.

"Oh," Tim said eagerly, "I almost forgot. I wanted to know if you have ever been to the farm?"

At that question, Father's eyes sparkled, "Oh yes," he said,

"Jeremy and I spent a wonderful vacation with the Mac-Neils when we were about twelve. For various reasons, we never did manage to get back there together, but we had a great time."

Well, that was more than enough for a son who trusted his dad. "All right," Tim chimed in again, "sounds like fun." And from back in the depths of the giant chair Sophie's blond head was bouncing up and down.

CHAPTER THREE

Off and Away

The days sped by and before they knew it, the morning of their departure had arrived. Dad would be driving them to the country and staying just long enough to introduce them to Mrs. MacNeil.

Tim was packed, and he had not forgotten the important things—his notebook, a sort of outdoor/survival journal he'd been keeping for the past couple of years; along with a

pair of binoculars from his last birthday. He had also managed to stuff in a few tattered nature guides.

Right beside her clothes, Sophie tucked in two small volumes
of poetry—she was just becoming interested in verses—and
then added a box of cards for writing home. Her favorite
green high-top "creek walking" boots fit into a large pocket
on the outside of her suitcase and presto, she was ready, too!

Before they left, Tim and Sophie hugged Kip and Sara, the
youngest of the Bigelows, and spent a bit more time talking
with their mother, giving her especially long squeezes.

All of a sudden Tim begged, "Mom, please don't forget to
feed Sammy and Digger."

Sammy, a tiger salamander, and Digger the frog were the
concessions Tim's parents had made to him, since right now

larger pets didn't fit in the picture. The salamander had come as a gift to him from an uncle who couldn't care for it anymore.

Mother pretended to shudder at the thought of the crickets and mealworms she'd be handling. Tim just laughed at her. He knew she wasn't really afraid. Mom loved Sammy and Digger too. She hugged Tim again, assuring him his pets would be fine, and said good-bye to the travelers one more time.

They joined their dad, who was waiting in the car, and away they went down the street, waving back and forth until they could no longer see their home.

At first the highway looked no different than it did near their own city, but by and by the buildings and houses became fewer and fewer, replaced with snow-covered hills and lots of trees.

They all listened to the entire dramatized Swiss Family Robinson on CD, and had sung quite a few rounds of song before Father passed through the small town of Hollis. Just as the last rousing chorus of their favorite camp song came to an end, he exited the highway, making a right turn onto a narrow dirt lane.

The road wound through some soft hills, sandy cliffs, and in and out of dense woods before beginning to drop into a narrow valley.

Since he knew what he was searching for, Father was the first one to glimpse the farm nestled near the valley floor. Following his dad's gaze, Tim cried, "I see it, down there—large red barns and a gigantic pond!"

Sophie saw the giant pond, too, and the three big barns and a beautiful farmhouse. "Yes, that's her house," said Father, "it's an old one."

Their car continued downhill till it came to a stop before two giant rock pillars that met above in an arch. Swinging from the top of the arch was a grayish-green sign, with scrolling letters and a bluebird in the corner, announcing they were now entering Misty Glen Farm.

Tim jumped out to open the gate, closing it as soon as Father pulled through, and still they continued along a tree-lined driveway.

Winter had stolen the leaves from these trees, but the sentinel trunks and the spread of the majestic branches were impressive to the children, nonetheless. Then, ever so slowly, the outline of the house they had spied earlier came into view.

As they grew near, Tim and Sophie saw a big two-story white house with green shutters and a long side porch—all of it neat and clean, with that well-cared-for look.

Tall pines mixed with white birches guarded the house on each side and they glimpsed tops of pines over the back of the house as well.

Shyly, Sophie found herself raising her hand in greeting to the small woman waving from the front porch, a black, tan, and white dog close by her side.

Jenny MacNeil was not very tall and she was not very large. She was just right, with her white hair pulled back gently into a soft bun, and an extraordinarily kind face.

As they pulled up to the house, the smiling woman and her dog approached them. Father jumped eagerly out of the car, even before the children, and greeted Mrs. MacNeil with an enthusiastic hug.

"Zach, it's so good to see you again!" she said as she returned his hug.

Tim and Sophie climbed out, too, stretching a bit from their ride. Father turned, saying, "Mrs. MacNeil, Tim and Sophie."

"Glad to meet you both," she said, giving Father's arm another happy hug. "It's good to have you back—you and your children!"

Then she dropped her hand to the dog at her side. "This is Tam. See that white spot on the top of his head?" She laughed, "It's like the Scottish hat, the tam o'shanter, and he loves to be petted."

Sophie, needing no further encouragement, fell on her knees in the snow, and, reaching out a hand to hold each side of Tam's silky face, she stared deeply into the dog's golden eyes.

Sophie's father had always appreciated her way with animals, and he smiled as he witnessed his daughter make yet another instant friend.

Meanwhile, Tim and Mrs. MacNeil glimpsed some low-flying ducks near the back of the yard and were busy discussing what species they might have been.

"Well," said Father, noting that everyone was looking quite happy, "it's time for me to leave if I'm to make a day trip of it." He set Tim and Sophie's suitcases near the porch, and, reaching out to hug his children, he told them how great he thought it was that they could spend their vacation with Mrs. MacNeil at Misty Glen Farm.

CHAPTER FOUR

Country Comforts

After the children retrieved their suitcases, Mrs. MacNeil ushered them up the front steps. "There are fresh oatmeal cookies in the kitchen, and milk, but first let me show you where your rooms will be. That's right, just follow me," she smiled warmly.

They entered a hall that went past a kitchen filled with delicious aromas, toward the living room and then up the stairs.

The old stairway itself was interesting. It went up eight steep steps to a sort of landing and then turned a corner and went up seven more. "I've always loved this staircase," Mrs. Mac-Neil said as they climbed, "it gives me a chance to stop and rest if I've a mind to."

They reached the second floor, and the children were surprised when they found themselves in a whole suite of rooms! Tim looked into his bedroom and saw rich wood paneling, warm plaid blankets tucked neatly into heavy wood bunks, and dark green curtains at the windows.

Sophie, stepping into her room, was delighted to discover white walls, pale green feather comforters, and a stack of colorful quilts for nights when the cold set in. "Oh…" she whispered softly as she noticed lace curtains at her window and reached out to touch a beautiful rose-painted lamp on the table beside the white iron bed. "This room is so pretty!"

She and Tim would be sharing a common bath situated in the middle with doors to each bedroom. Across the hall they were pleased to see an inviting sitting room with comfortable couches, chairs, a round game table, and plenty of lamps. On the far side of the room stood a big oak desk and several tall bookcases, half-filled with books. The corner opposite the bookcases held a built-in gas fireplace, whose cheerful flame made even the big drafty second floor feel warm and cozy.

"You are always welcome to be downstairs," Mrs. MacNeil quickly assured them, "in the living room or the kitchen, anywhere in the house you wish. But, when you want a bit of time by yourself, this is your own place to enjoy. Now, how about unpacking a little later and let's find those warm cookies?"

They descended the stairs still talking, and Tim asked Mrs. MacNeil about the man who helped her on the farm. "Oh, you mean Barney. He had business to take care of in Illinois.

He'll be gone for at least a week, maybe a little more, but he should return before you leave. You'll enjoy meetin' each other, I know you will," she promised as she rounded the corner toward the kitchen. Tim gave Sophie the thumbs-up and they shook their heads in amazement. The choice to spend their winter holidays with Mrs. MacNeil was looking like a good one—far better, in fact, than they'd ever imagined!

Later that night, full of oatmeal cookies, the soft chewy kind loaded with dried cherries, the children made their way upstairs. They found their pajamas and toothbrushes and it wasn't long before they were nestled into deep soft beds, drifting slowly off to sleep with smiles on their faces, listening to a chorus of owls talk back and forth across the distant woods.

CHAPTER FIVE

Waking Up at Misty Glen

It would be morning before the unpacking was finished. The sun was just sneaking through the windows when the children awoke and it took a minute for them to remember where they were.

Then Tim called out to Sophie and she came running into his room, hopped on the bed, and began pulling the covers around her shoulders. "Did you hear the owls last night?" Tim asked his sister.

"Oh yes," Sophie cried, "I knew that's what they were! They were magnificent, weren't they?"

"Yeah, owls are great! I bet we hear a lot more of them and maybe some coyotes or even a wolf. Right now, let's unpack and get dressed, then we can go find Mrs. MacNeil."

Sophie was already headed for the door, eager to put her things away and dress for the day.

They hung their clothes in the giant wardrobes, tucking their folded items into the drawers underneath. Sophie planned to take her boots downstairs, so she set them near the door. They stacked the reading books and a few favorite games they'd brought with them on one of the empty bookcase shelves in the sitting room and Sophie completed her unpacking by placing her note cards and pens on the oak desktop.

Then she tumbled into jeans and a sweater and finished with warm socks and shoes. Tim dressed, too, and they went downstairs together.

Breakfast was waiting for them in the dining room. Mrs. MacNeil had set steaming bowls of oatmeal, and toast made from homemade bread, on the table.

Now, Tim had never been overly fond of oatmeal. Politely, he picked up his spoon; hesitantly, he tried it. This was wonderful! What had Mrs. MacNeil done? Sophie was also eating with delight when their hostess came into the room. Tim and Sophie looked up at her. "How did you make this oatmeal so delicious?" they both wanted to know at once.

Mrs. MacNeil laughed out loud. "Well, I'm so glad you like it," she said, still grinning. "My husband, John, and I loved oatmeal. We would have gladly eaten it every day. But we noticed many years ago that children often don't care for it quite as much as we did. When your father and Jeremy came to visit one summer, I had to develop some tricks to help the oatmeal mornings along. So, I use some fresh chopped apples, a little brown sugar, butter, and some cinnamon. Well, next time I make it I'll just show you how I do it."

As the children scraped their bowls and ladled huge spoonfuls of strawberry jam onto their toast, Sophie remembered she'd left her boots upstairs.

"There are plenty of boots, all sizes, on the back porch," Aunt Jenny assured Sophie.

"Thanks; I'll borrow some this time and get mine when I'm up next."

After breakfast was over, the children helped wash the dishes and put them away. Sophie enjoyed the glass-front cupboards where the dishes were visible: china cups, plates, teapots and bowls—all in a softly faded pink pattern. Reaching into the cupboard, she picked up a cup and turned it upside down. On the bottom was written Johnson Bros., England. She set it down gently and reached for another cup to dry.

When everything was tidy, Mrs. MacNeil showed them around the rest of the house and then the barns, stopping now and then at various points of interest.

It was out near the orchard that Tim and Sophie first met Esmerelda, the velvety brown Jersey cow—milk provider for the farm. Milking and caring for Esmy was the sole duty of Mrs. MacNeil as well as her particular love. She never minded getting up early, summer or winter, and milking in the quiet barn before the sun came up. And the nightly routine of milking and feeding the cow was, for her, the calm benediction to each evening. "Esmy and I have an understanding," Aunt Jenny said. "We do very well together."

As they kept walking, they reached the field near the middle barn and Mrs. MacNeil introduced them to Donny, the towering Percheron. Seeing Donny, Sophie burst out, "Oh, so you *do* still have the big gray horse Daddy remembered!" Calmly wrapping an arm around one massive leg, she continued, "He said you'd raised it from a baby. I just know he was darling when he was little."

"Yes," replied Mrs. MacNeil, grateful for Donny's forbearing patience. She gently repositioned Sophie's arm, showing her instead how to stroke his neck. "But, a Percheron baby is still quite large." Mrs. MacNeil shook her head, and, smiling, remarked, "We sure had our hands full in those days."

Finally, she took them to meet the chickens and showed Tim and Sophie how they were fed and the best way to gather eggs.

Because Barney was away, the three put their heads together and made a plan for who was to be responsible, and when, to gather eggs or to feed the chickens, and to put Donny up and feed him at night.

Tim and Sophie were delighted with each new experience, and this was only the beginning of their MacNeil farm days.

Well Laid Plans

The winter ice sat thick on the branches, and the birds were making a good show, nipping up all the seeds the kind woman had left. Their short, grateful chirps could be heard clear to the back of the yard where the breeze was just beginning to stir the pines.

Tim and Sophie listened to the birds and felt the fresh wind as they neared the pasture fence. They were just returning from a late afternoon hike, and since Barney was still away, they were also bringing Donny in for the night.

Reaching out, Tim pushed at the weathered wood, and, creaking softly, the gate swung wide. Together he and Sophie led the huge gray horse into the paddock and up toward the barn. All the time they were in such a deep discussion about what they had just seen that Sophie almost forgot to close and latch the gate.

"But, Tim," piped Sophie excitedly as she opened the stall door for Donny to enter, "how do we know that what we saw was real?"

Tim scooped up a measure of grain and poured it into the feeding bin as Sophie filled the water bucket. "I don't know, but I sure do want to see it again up close!" He broke off a couple of flakes of hay and tossed them into the stall.

"Same here," Sophie replied, resting her hand flat on the horse's warm head while he ate. "So, what are our plans?"

"Well, Mrs. MacNeil will be wanting us for supper soon and it's getting dark."

"Isn't there a full moon tonight?"

"Yeah, but it's going to get bitter cold. I think we'd best wait till morning."

"Okay," said Sophie, "then we can go ahead and explore the south hills after we've checked out what we saw this afternoon."

"We could go right after breakfast," Tim mused. "Hey! Maybe Mrs. McNeil will let us pack a lunch to take with us. I mean, the way she cares for all those little birds, surely she'll help us out as well."

And so the plans were laid.

CHAPTER SEVEN

Preparations for Exploring

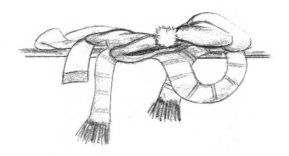

Morning arrived clear and sparkling, and though it was still very cold, the sun made it seem much warmer than the night. Sophie and Tim bounded into the kitchen early, before the stove had time to warm up the large room with its yellow painted walls and dark aged wood.

Mrs. MacNeil was busy, taking warm muffins out of the pan and humming to herself, when she heard the children come in.

"Morning! What a bright-ish day and just the thing for two children who want explorin'! There won't be any snow to-day," laughed the small woman.

Tim and Sophie looked at each other. "How did you know we wanted to go exploring today?" asked Sophie.

"Oh, my stars," chuckled Mrs. MacNeil, "you've been riding the horse, you've spied out most of the nooks and crevices of this big old house and you've been on a hike. Now is the time to do some real exploring—uncharted territory, you know!"

"Well," Sophie replied, "we were thinking of taking off across the fields toward the south hills. We haven't done much ex-ploring there—along the cliffs and woods. It might take most of the day, so we were wondering if we might pack some food for our lunch?"

Before Sophie had even finished speaking, the generous woman was grabbing up loaves of bread and pieces of meat, as well as yellow cheese and firm red apples. "Of course you may," she said as she sliced off cheese and meat, pared apples, and tucked substantial sandwiches, along with huge sugar cookies, into a brown leather bag.

"Here is an old thermos with a good working cork. You can pour in water or milk and there will be enough for you both," said Mrs. MacNeil, her cheerful enthusiasm filling Tim and Sophie with excitement and gratitude.

"Do remember to be wise. Wear two pair of socks and put a spare pair in your pocket in case you get the others wet. Take your gloves and scarves, and wear a sweater or two under your coats. Your mother and father would be so disappointed in me if I let you become ill."

"Thank you, Mrs. MacNeil," said Sophie.

"Yes, thanks!" echoed Tim.

Tim and Sophie planned to do exactly as Mrs. MacNeil had suggested. Around the corner and up the stairs they raced. Once in their rooms, they made their beds and spruced up the bathroom by straightening the towels, rinsing out the sink, and wiping clean the old mirror that hung over it.

In their sitting room, Sophie and Tim put away a few stray game pieces, matching them up to their boxes.

Surveying their work, they agreed that everything was in its place and since this was their free day from any farm chores, they could get started right away. But first they had to dress for the cold!

It took some time to bundle themselves up. Sophie started laughing as she tugged at the second pair of socks. "This second pair just doesn't slide on as easily as the first," she giggled, then added, "Don't forget to take that extra pair for your coat pocket."

This time Sophie remembered to grab her own boots, and boots in hand, she followed Tim downstairs to the glassed-in back porch where their coats, hats, mittens, and scarves were waiting.

Tim struggled for a moment to get his coat over the two sweaters he had on, but finding the side tabs that loosened the coat, he breathed a sigh of relief.

When everything was ready, he and Sophie returned to the kitchen. Opening up the lunch sack, Tim managed to squeeze into the already bulging bag his binoculars, notebook, and pencil. Then he picked up the bag and shrugged it onto his shoulder.

Mrs. MacNeil turned from the counter and handed each of them an orange-nut muffin. "This'll do for your breakfast and hold you till lunch," she laughed. "I know you are eager to be on your way," and waving good-bye to the adventurers, she scooted them out the door.

It had taken awhile, but at last here they were, a brother and sister from the city, setting off for an entire day of exploring in the dazzling Michigan countryside!

CHAPTER EIGHT

From the Top of the Trestle

They really did intend to go toward the south, into the woods and cliffs and winding frozen streams, but first they were in a hurry to take another quick look at what they had seen, or at least thought they had seen, the day before.

"Do you remember where the bridge is?" Sophie asked her brother.

"Well, not exactly, but I think if we keep moving to the east we'll come across something familiar."

They kept plodding forward and it was sometime later when they emerged from the thick woods. Up ahead, at the top of the slope, Tim finally spotted the long-abandoned railroad bridge. A reminder of Michigan's logging past, the rickety trestle traversed the stony creek bed that ran across the MacNeil property.

Yesterday, the afternoon light had turned to dusk, and what with the shadows, the children had seen only part of something that looked valuable on the creek bank below. A few moments more and they would find out!

Placing their feet tentatively, step by step, they moved onto the weathered old trestle frame, and looking down they could almost see what they had strained so hard to identify in yesterday's twilight. Just a bit further out onto the trestle, and again they peered down among the rocks below.

Yes, there it was! In the bright morning light, they could clearly make out a green canvas bag lodged between two large stones, and what appeared to be several gold coins that had spilled from the mouth of the bag.

However, in their excitement, neither Tim nor Sophie heard the chunks of ice-covered stones sliding aside as a dark tall figure loomed up behind them.

CHAPTER NINE

Down, Down, Down

Without warning, rough hands grasped Sophie and Tim by their jackets and jerked them from the trestle, back to the rocky railroad right-of-way.

"What are you doing here? This isn't your place!" the voice was low and gruff.

Sophie's eyes went wide with fear. Instantly Tim knew he

had to be calm enough for both of them, so, trying to sound casual, he replied, "Sorry, mister, we didn't know...we were just out taking a morning walk."

The man towering over them was dressed like a farmer, but Tim had not seen him anywhere before.

Less agitated now, the stranger said, "You kids keep away from here, understand?"

They nodded and he released them both, figuring they had not yet had time to see what lay beneath the old train trestle.

Sophie and Tim made a quick retreat back into the woods, but as soon as they reached a spot of safety they stopped to talk.

"We need to go back," said Tim, "and find a way to get some

of the coins. If we take them to Mrs. MacNeil, she'll know what to do. Let's get a little farther away. We'll eat our lunch and then decide what to do next."

"OK," Sophie answered softly, though anyone could see that she was considerably more nervous than Tim at the whole idea of returning.

With their backs to the man and the trestle, they traveled over the hill and toward some sheltering pines. Not too far into the woods, they found a gathering of large stumps in the sunshine.

Brushing the light snow off, they settled themselves on the widest two and burrowed into the bag of sandwiches. As they ate, Tim began to talk with his sister about how to accomplish their goal.

"We'll have to approach quietly and make sure the man is gone."

"But how are we going to get the coins?"

"Well, we'll have to find a safe way to get down into the creek bed. That is—if the coins are still there."

They continued to eat and for a moment forgot everything except the lunch Mrs. MacNeil had provided. The sandwiches were delicious and the cookies and milk, just right. They agreed to save the apples and cheese for a snack on the way home, and, shaking out the wrappings, Sophie scattered the last of the bread crumbs onto the ground for the birds.

"I think," said Tim as he pulled out his notebook and pencil, "we should make a map of where the railroad trestle is, and exactly where on the bank we saw the bag and the coins."

Glancing up from her task, Sophie nodded, "And, a good description of that man we saw!"

So they did, drawing the location of the bridge and the spot from the creek bank where they saw the treasure. Tim kept writing in his notebook and they included as many details as they could remember about the man: his size, height and weight, and the features of his face, eyes, nose, and mouth.

"Don't forget to put in the part about that crooked little scar on his lip," Sophie reminded him.

Tim noted the scar and finished with, "man wearing dark jeans, blue plaid shirt, canvas work jacket, brown, square-toed boots. Had a deep bass voice."

Tim tucked the notebook and pencil in his jacket pocket, buttoned the flap, and ducked his head through the strap of the binoculars. When he'd picked up the lunch sack, the two retraced their steps, keeping a keen lookout for the stranger. But, they saw no one, even though now and then Tim would take the binoculars and scan the woods and clearing, patiently and thoroughly all around them as they advanced, until they were nearly to the bridge.

"Hold up a minute, Soph, this bag feels all lopsided." Tim removed the leather bag, replaced the binoculars in it, and rearranged the thermos, moving it to the top to distribute the weight. "That's better."

Then they stepped forward once more and soon they were back at the trestle. Glancing a bit nervously around them, the children moved out onto the weathered bridge to see if the bag and coins were still there.

Suddenly there was a sharp crack! Several of the ancient

boards split and began to slip sideways. With nothing left to stand on, the children slid beneath the rails and began to fall. They continued falling and sliding about nine feet down the slope to the rocky creek bank below, spilling their lunch sack, thermos—everything—as they went.

Fortunately, a few stout bushes helped break their fall, and most of their belongings landed within a few feet of them. Only the thermos was truly lost, the glass liner shattering noisily as it hit one of the largest rocks below.

Miraculously, neither of the children was hurt, but both were badly frightened. When the first shock wore off, they realized that they had landed only feet from the green canvas bag and the loose gold coins. Carefully, Tim moved out over several slippery, snow-covered rocks and touched the old bag, discovering that it was, indeed, filled with money.

With some effort, he pried several of the gold coins out of the frozen mud and handed one to Sophie. Wiping the mud from the coin with her thumbs, she turned the gold piece over, examining both sides.

She could not make sense of any of the words, save the word "God," and the date, 1879. There seemed to be a picture of a girl on one side of it and some kind of a crown and a lion with a sword on the other.

Tim left the bag where he found it, but placed two coins in his pocket and, of course, Sophie had hers.

As they gathered their belongings and looked around, they made an alarming discovery. The creek walls were much steeper than they had appeared from above. The sharp, icy rock-covered sides that surrounded them prevented any easy way out, and the trestle from which they had fallen was too high for either of them to reach, even standing on each other's shoulders. The creek was also quite deep.

Trapped by several feet of icy water on one side, and a nearly vertical wall of loose boulders on the other side, the children looked in all directions, "Oh, Tim!" cried Sophie, "we can't get out!"

Thinking quickly, Tim soothed, "Don't panic, Soph, we'll make lots of noise. Someone will hear us," and praying that the stranger was by now miles away, Tim and Sophie began to call and whistle, eager to arouse someone's help.

CHAPTER TEN

The Wagon and the Rope

The wagon groaned softly to a stop and the driver climbed to the ground. The figure waited a moment, listening, gaining bearings, then on a hunch reached for the thickly coiled rope in the back of the wagon.

Slinging an arm through the circle of rope and heaving it over her shoulder, Mrs. MacNeil moved hastily into the woods with Tam following along beside her. She veered toward the last sounds she'd heard—whistles, she thought. It had sounded like someone might be in trouble.

Emerging at last from the woods into the clearing near the old logging trestle, she began to make out voices as Tam ran ahead.

"Hallo there, where are you?"

"Careful, Mrs. MacNeil!" yelled Tim. "The trestle is broken. We fell through! We're down the slope at the creek."

"Thanks for the warning," she called, trying not to sound alarmed, as she gave Tam who was whining and sniffing near the slope, the command to "lay!"

"I'll be careful, and I'll have you out in no time," she encouraged.

Deftly she tied the rope around a tree with a clove hitch, thankful that her husband had taught her such a valuable skill, and with the loose end in tow, she crept carefully toward the slippery edge of the bank.

Mrs. MacNeil called down to the children, "I'm not able to pull you up myself, but I'm throwing down this rope. I've tied a few knots for footholds—the end is well secured to that giant oak. It's okay," she persuaded, "just come up one at a time. You can pull yourselves out."

Tim tightened the lunch bag on his shoulder, reached out for the rope, and came up first, quite easily. Then he bent to help and encourage his sister as she made her ascent. Once, Sophie slipped and it was Tim's calm voice saying, "That's all right Soph; rest a second and try again," that gave her confidence to reach the top.

Soon they were out of the deep, stony crevice, and Mrs. Mc-Neil was untying the rope at the tree as the children tried to brush some of the mud and snow from their pants.

"Well, that came in real handy," she murmured as she automatically began to loop the rope over her shoulder. But the moment she turned to face Sophie and Tim, she found them racing right into her arms!

CHAPTER ELEVEN

Aunt Jenny

Letting the rope fall to the ground, she gathered the children up and squeezed them both tightly for several seconds like they were long-lost family. "Whew!" she said, breathless. "I think now, if you like, you might start calling me 'Aunt Jenny!'"

"Yes!" agreed Tim and Sophie, hugging her back with all their might. After awhile Tim set down the lunch sack and looked to see what damage had been done in the fall. The apples were squashed and he left them on the ground, but the binoculars seemed to work fine and Tim breathed a sigh of relief.

However, there was the corked bottle that had fallen from the bag. Tim and Sophie were genuinely sorry as they apologized and recounted their fall.

"Never you mind," Aunt Jenny said quickly, "the important thing is that you're safe and we're together! Maybe tomorrow we can come back and look over this situation. You can tell me all about it—sure looks mysterious to me, but right now I have the strongest feeling that we should get out of here. Let's go back to the farm. When we're sure the animals have all been properly cared for, we'll find some hot supper for ourselves."

Sophie and Tim could hardly believe their ears. Aunt Jenny

wasn't mad! She wasn't mad about the accident. She wasn't mad about her lost thermos—she wasn't mad about anything! And she actually wanted to come back and help them figure out the mystery. Again they gave her quick hugs, and as soon as Tim picked up the bag, the three of them set off through the woods to the clearing where Jenny MacNeil had left the wagon.

Tim assisted her into the wagon and held out his hand to help his sister, who was still shaking a bit from her fright. Then he pulled himself up beside Sophie while Tam sprang into the back, and Aunt Jenny turned the wagon in a wide arc toward the house.

CHAPTER TWELVE

Whence Came the Coins?

As they jostled along in the wagon, Aunt Jenny kept looking over at the children asking, "Are you sure you two are all right? Are you hurting anywhere?"

Sophie crinkled her eyes in a shaky laugh and declared, "With all those warm clothes you asked us to wear, we pretty much bounced like a ball! I probably don't even have a bruise."

Tim pointed out a tiny scratch on her cheek, to which Sophie replied, "Well, that would be the only part of me that wasn't multi-layered!"

They all laughed, and Tim assured her he was okay, as well, but promised Aunt Jenny that they'd both take a better inventory when they got back to the farm.

"Before we feed the animals, there's going to be some strong tea with milk and sugar for you two…'to put the feet back under ye,'" Aunt Jenny vowed with passion.

Then she sighed, "Mercy, I think I'll have a cup, myself!"

Relieved and finally satisfied, Aunt Jenny was curious, "Tim, how did you two happen to get into that fix, anyway?"

"Yesterday afternoon," Tim confessed, "we were hiking and

discovered the railway bridge. We walked a little way out on it and looked down at the creek below. Sophie saw something." His sister piped in, "I saw a sack-like thing wedged in the rocks and something that looked like coins."

"I told Sophie the reason we couldn't see it very well was because it was becoming so dark, and we decided we'd better get home."

"So, Tim and I thought we'd come back this morning and quickly check it out before we explored the land over to the south." Sophie ended quietly, "We didn't say anything because we weren't sure that what we had seen was real."

Suddenly, Tim remembered that they hadn't shown Aunt Jenny the coins. He reached into his pocket and drew out one of the pieces. "Look at this!"

Aunt Jenny gazed at the coin and then looked at the children in amazement.

"Well, this is an interesting find."

"What is it?" inquired Sophie.

"It's hard to tell for sure, certainly while I'm driving, but the money is foreign and old. It may be valuable as gold, and possibly as an antiquity."

"An-what?" asked Sophie.

Aunt Jenny laughed, "Antiquity, a thing which is old and has historic value."

"Oh, that's good I guess," said Sophie.

"We met a man near the trestle," Tim said. "He scared Sophie, but when I told him we were just out for a walk, he seemed nicer." Aunt Jenny just listened quietly, making careful note of all that they said. "By the way," queried Tim, interrupting her train of thought, "how did you ever find us?"

"Well, as Providence would have it," Aunt Jenny said, "I was just returning from visiting a neighbor, and I heard that magnificent whistle of yours. Of course I didn't know whose whistle it was!

"I just thought somebody might be wantin' some help, but I had to leave the wagon—I couldn't drive it through the woods. At the last minute I did think to grab the rope and then Tam and I came searching. When I made it to the bridge, I was certainly surprised to discover it was you!"

The children were beginning to realize the real danger in not being where they had said they would be, and again they told Aunt Jenny they were sorry. "Well, I'm thankful it all worked out—and you'll do just right the next time," she said. Amazement shone in Tim and Sophie's eyes. "Thank you, Aunt Jenny, and thank you for finding us!

Later, hungrily eating thick beefy stew, and tender brown bread that Aunt Jenny had made herself, the three talked over the situation. Mulling over the events, Aunt Jenny muttered quietly, "Whence came the coins?"

"Whence?" Sophie said.

"Oh, it means 'where.' I was just thinking, how do you suppose that bag of money became stuck in the rocks at the side of the creek?"

Tim, who had finished spreading thick butter all over his

bread, licked his fingers and replied, "I don't know; maybe that guy we saw had something to do with it. But he disappeared and we didn't ever see him again."

Meanwhile, supper came to an end with a deep pan of blueberry pie and a pitcher of fresh milk.

Thinking back on their day, Sophie and Tim wondered at the unfolding events, completely grateful for their rescue and fully satisfied by their dinner.

Everything was looking more promising. And, they had ten days left! But still…there was that matter of the stranger… and what he might do if he came back and discovered they had returned.

CHAPTER THIRTEEN

The Knock at the Door

In the morning Aunt Jenny seemed tired, so for lunch Tim and Sophie made her sandwiches, along with water for tea boiled up in the kettle on the old stove.

The kettle itself was also ancient, but it bubbled cheerfully, and the children poured out hot cups for themselves as well. Then they all settled down for a quiet meal. Bang! There was a loud knock at the door. Jumping in surprise, Sophie clinked her cup hard against the saucer as Tam bristled and growled. A look and a gesture from Aunt Jenny quieted him, and obediently Tam dropped to the carpet, though he kept his eyes riveted on the door.

Cautiously, Mrs. MacNeil asked the children to wait right there while she went to see who it was. A man Aunt Jenny did not recognize was standing on the steps. With a deep demanding voice, he began to ask after any children that might be about.

Mrs. MacNeil straightened herself to full height and replied indignantly, "Who are you? Why do you want to know?"

Suddenly, a dark look came into the man's eyes and he said more viciously, "It doesn't matter, but if you know what's good for you, you'll keep them kids where you can see 'em." Then he turned and sped away.

Tim and Sophie could hear the conversation down the hallway and they recognized the voice. They agreed it was time to tell Aunt Jenny more about their meeting with this man.

As Mrs. MacNeil returned, Tim drew his notebook out of his pocket. "Aunt Jenny, we wrote all this down after that guy caught us at the bridge," and Tim shared with her all the descriptions they had recorded.

She listened carefully, and finally convinced that the man they described was the same man who had just knocked at her door, she walked straight into the kitchen to dial the phone.

Dale Lane, the county sheriff, had been a family friend of the MacNeils for many years. Jenny knew she could turn to him whenever she needed help and she thought now might just be the time. She spoke with him for a few minutes before she hung up.

"Well," she told the children, "the sheriff's office is beginning an investigation of this man. We have a clear description, and your coins for evidence, but Dale would like to go slowly and see if he can catch this stranger 'red-handed,' so to speak."

"I have a question." Tim said. "Is that trestle—the bridge— on your property? The man told us that it wasn't our place."

Aunt Jenny quickly assured Tim that the old railroad bridge and the creek, as well as some of the land surrounding it, was MacNeil property. "We have 320 acres and hold the first rights to 320 more on the periphery. That man was trespassing, but Dale will look into everything for us."

As the three perched on the edge of the sofa and chairs, Mrs. MacNeil asked, "I know I said that we'd all go back and look things over, but don't you think it's important, in light of all the events, that we should let Dale do his own investigating?"

It didn't take much convincing for Tim and Sophie to see the wisdom in this idea. From the moment the man had shown up right at their own door, they'd lost all interest in returning to the bridge, and they agreed wholeheartedly.

CHAPTER FOURTEEN

What Happens in Town

Hitched up to the wagon, the Percheron stood with classic patience as he waited for Aunt Jenny. Now, Aunt Jenny loved driving the wagon to town more than most people loved driving their cars and trucks, yet the children knew she did own a vehicle. They'd seen a truck in the garage beside the barn. It was a restored dark green Chevy from the early 1950s and it had "Misty Glen Farm Vegetables" painted on the sides.

Still, most of the time, Mrs. MacNeil drove the wagon. Usually, she said, she could choose when she wanted to go visiting, so weather wasn't a problem, and by now the children understood her passion for being out in the fresh air regardless of sunshine or clouds.

Today, solid gray clouds were darkening and beginning to drop lower in the sky. "I can almost smell snow," Aunt Jenny predicted. "It's coming...perhaps tomorrow." She was also sure today's cold would not turn bitter and that their coats would provide plenty of warmth for their trip to town.

When everyone was loaded, Aunt Jenny gave a cluck and the wagon started with a gentle jerk as plumes of Donny's breath floated back and mixed with those of the riders.

The journey to the small town of Hollis, only two miles away, took about half an hour through countryside that was so interesting both children kept exclaiming and pointing out one thing or another until they had reached the outskirts of the village.

There they stopped near an abandoned building on the edge of town.

Aunt Jenny unhitched the wagon and tied Donny up to an old fence. "This will provide some protection for both the horse and the wagon away from the cars. Wait just a minute; I need to give Donny a chance to drink," she said as she took the cover off a water bucket that had been lashed to the back of the wagon.

After she was finished, the three moved up the sidewalk and turned toward the general store. The door was just clicking shut behind them when Derk Klassen, the owner, appeared and greeted Jenny. She stopped to talk with him while the children looked around.

Finding the aisle of toys, it didn't take long for Tim to choose a heavy, metal farm tractor, painted green for Kip, one with working parts, while his sister selected a deep, plush stuffed horse, dapple-gray—the same color as Donny. Sophie knew Sara would be delighted with the horse as she and Sara both loved animals.

Before they paid for their presents, they added packages of gum for Kip and Sara, and a plastic model dog for themselves, one that looked like Tam, to remember him by.

When they had given Mr. Klassen their money, and he had wrapped the gifts and put them in a brown bag, they all eagerly set off up the street to the home of Sam Bern, the coin man.

CHAPTER FIFTEEN

Sam Bern the Coin Man

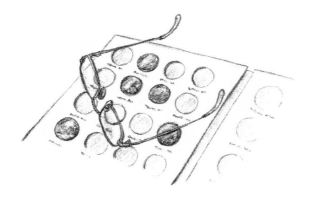

Sam greeted them at the door and helped them hang up their coats on the curved metal hooks in the entry. Then he led them down a long hall lined with old framed photographs to a back room. "Jenny, why don't you take this chair? It's a bit more comfortable. Tim and Sophie, you may use the chairs in front of my desk."

As they sat, they began to look around, noticing books and

papers scattered everywhere, and several packages of coins lying open on the desk.

"I don't consider myself an expert," Mr. Bern began, peering over his gold-rimmed glasses, "but I have been studying coins for many years. I enjoy collecting, and I'd be glad to try to help you if I can."

"Here's what we found!" said Tim and Sophie, eagerly offering up their coins for inspection. Sam looked them over carefully, and gradually he grew more interested.

"Obviously, you already know how old these coins are by the date, but I think there is more we can learn. It is my guess that they are probably not from a collector or museum."

"How can you tell?" asked Sophie.

"Coins from a fine collection or a museum would each be carefully placed in a sealed plastic case."

"Oh, I've seen some of those," said Tim.

"Yes, like this one," said Mr. Bern, pulling a case from his top drawer and handing it around for Sophie and Mrs. MacNeil to see.

"But, not all of your coins are sealed up like that," observed Sophie.

"That's right," agreed Mr. Bern, "the plastic cases, called slabs, are used on more valuable coins, to help prevent moisture and dirt particles from getting in and causing corrosion, and so the pieces don't become nicked.

"On the other hand, coins that have been knocking together in a bag will have marks and other signs of wear, as these seem to have.

"That's why I don't think they've been appraised. I think the ones you found might have been lost or hidden away for a time and someone just recently discovered them. They probably have not yet been seen by a coin collector because I think they could be valuable and might well have been slabbed to protect them.

"How large did you say the bag was? Though I suppose there could have been other kinds of coins in it...hmm, let me look these up in my books." He turned to pull a couple of volumes off the shelf behind his chair and before he even began to thumb the pages, he said, "I can tell you right now that the writing is Dutch."

He stopped talking to read for a moment. Then he said, "Look, these coins are called Wilhelmina...see the figure of the young girl on the front?" and he turned the book toward them.

"It matches the picture on the ones we found!" Tim said excitedly, as Mr. Bern returned the coins to the children.

"It says here that she was only seventeen, but she was the queen...the back of the coin has the Dutch royal crest with a crown and…" Just then a shadow passed the window and Tim and Sophie were startled as they glimpsed the profile of a man's face—a familiar face. Tim rushed to the window, but he could see nothing. Mr. Bern hurriedly pulled the drapes shut while Aunt Jenny made another call to the sheriff.

CHAPTER SIXTEEN

Officially Investigated

"Dale? This is Jenny MacNeil. I just wanted you to know that I think someone may be following us." She briefly related the scene at Sam's office while Dale listened. Then Aunt Jenny took in the sheriff's instructions, nodded her head, and hung up the receiver with a satisfied click.

"Well, now we are part of the official investigation," she said, and added, "the sheriff said to keep to our activities and he would tail us. We won't see him. He'll keep out of sight. So, I guess we just continue with our plans and try to stay calm, though that may not be too easy," she laughed.

Despite her concerns, it wasn't long before everyone was fully absorbed in speculations over the coins, who they might belong to, the fact that they were Dutch, and how the bag happened to be at the bottom of the old bridge.

All at once, Mr. Bern, who had been looking through his books, marked his place and turned to show Tim, Sophie and Aunt Jenny the information he'd found.

"Wilhelmina coin, an alloy minted in 1879 in Holland. Since we know the year the coin was made, we can also learn about some of the things that were happening in that period of history in Holland—immigrations and such. Maybe that's how the coins came to America. You know, a lot of the Dutch settled right here in Michigan."

Then Mr. Bern continued, "It will take me a little time to finish all the information that's listed here."

"You should keep one of these for further research," Tim suggested, as he handed one of his coins back to Mr. Bern.

Sam took the coin, "Thank you, I'll take very good care of it," and he put it in a small plastic bag. Then it was time for them to leave.

Mrs. MacNeil and the children thanked Mr. Bern for helping

them, and set off down the hall to gather their coats.

"You're welcome," said Sam as they reached the front door, "but I'm the one who should be thanking you." At their inquiring glances, he explained, with a wave of his hand, "For letting me in on your mysterious find!"

CHAPTER SEVENTEEN

Lunch at the Diner

Only when Aunt Jenny, Tim, and Sophie were outside on the sidewalk did they remember there might be someone following them. Then, feeling self-conscious and trying not to look around, they endeavored to act as natural as possible as they rounded the corner and walked up to the diner for some lunch.

The Hollis Diner was, in part, an old-fashioned soda shop. Sitting on stools at the counter, the trio ordered cheeseburgers, fries, and onion rings that arrived in black plastic baskets lined with white paper. Aunt Jenny surprised them with ice cream sodas.

Despite the scare in Mr. Bern's office, they talked and joked, and blew the paper off the straws at each other, agreeing that Aunt Jenny was the best shot.

"I've just had more practice," she admitted with merry eyes.

During a break in their conversation, the door of the diner opened and a young woman with twins came walking in. Sophie watched the toddlers playing for a moment. As she turned back, she noticed Aunt Jenny openly watching as well.

"Dad told us that you and Mr. MacNeil didn't have children, but you seem to love kids so much," Sophie observed gently.

"No, we couldn't have children of our own," Aunt Jenny said softly, and then stronger as her memories warmed, "fortunately for us, my sister lived close by. She had three—two boys and a girl. We spent lots of time with them. My sister's whole family and John and I often vacationed together. In the summer we swam in the pond, and the three little ones had over-nights quite often. We loved having them near."

"Where are they now?" Tim asked.

"The children were older when my sister's family moved to Arizona for her husband's business, and they've all stayed there, even though they're grown up and have families of their own. Once every couple of years I fly west to see them." Aunt Jenny's eyes gleamed, "It's pure delightful pandemonium to see my sister and her husband, along with my niece and nephews and all of their children gathered together!"

Tim, who had been listening, smiled at the thought of Aunt Jenny driving her horse and wagon one day, and then flying across the country the next.

As they continued to eat lunch, they talked about their favorite topics—books, nature, and sports, and the children listened to Aunt Jenny tell them more about the town and the farm until everyone was finished. Tim and Sophie climbed down from the tall stools, gathered up their packages, and waited while Aunt Jenny paid the man at the register.

Then Tim held the door open and they were back on the sidewalk. It looked like a typical day—a few cars, a bicycle or two passing by. There didn't seem to be anything unusual. They just kept walking, and soon they were back at the wagon.

While the children put their purchases in the back, Aunt Jenny prepared a small amount of oats and grain for the horse.

Due to their early departure, Donny had not spent his usual time grazing on the morning hay flakes in his stall.

So, as soon as Sophie held out the feedbag, Donny stuck his big head deep down and came up with a great mouthful. He crunched so slowly and happily that Tim laughed.

"He seems to be enjoying his meal as much as we did our hamburgers and sodas."

Of course, Donny continued to eat, and he certainly wasn't in any hurry. Eventually, though, the bag was empty. Aunt Jenny hitched him up, untied the wagon, and pointed it toward Misty Glen Farm.

However, this time the ride home was rather quiet, each traveler silently contemplating his own thoughts about the day, the coins, and the shadowy face they had seen at the window.

Aunt Jenny was also thinking to herself, "I'm glad Barney is coming home."

The Story of Barney Owen

The dirt road turn-off was in sight when Aunt Jenny broke into their thoughts to tell Tim and Sophie more about Barney.

"Barney is due back this afternoon."

"We'll get to meet him?" asked Tim excitedly.

"Of course," smiled Aunt Jenny and then she began to laugh, remembering how Barney had first come to her farm. "Barney Owen sort of ran into me," she chuckled.

"Oh, tell us the story!" begged Sophie, tugging gently on Aunt Jenny's sleeve.

"Well, late one afternoon, six months or so after my husband's funeral, I was sitting in the living room reading the newspaper when I heard a knock at the door. I opened the screen and beheld a sandy-haired young man—quite slender and tall—dressed in overalls, and wearing a baseball cap.

"He quietly informed me that he had swerved to miss an animal and had crashed into our fence.

"'It's broken...about six feet of it,' he admitted sadly, then confessed, 'I'm between jobs at the moment, traveling across the state, and I don't have enough cash to reimburse you for the damage.'

"I did have the presence of mind to ask him if he was okay, and if his car was badly damaged," remembered Aunt Jenny.

"He told me that he was fine, and his car had a dent but it wasn't important.

"By then I could tell he was embarrassed and I realized that he could have easily driven off without ever bothering to stop and apologize or to try to make amends. So I asked him if he knew how to fix the fence himself. Glancing shyly from under his cap he said, 'I guess so,' and added, 'I'm not afraid of work.'

"That well-mended fence proved to be the beginning of all that he's done for Misty Glen Farm. I just keep finding more things for him to do and he stays on."

"Then, having Barney's help turned out to be good for you," said Tim.

"Oh, my, yes! He loves growing things almost as much as my husband did, and he's real good at what he does. We've worked this farm together for the past five years, and I count on Barney for many things that I can no longer do."

"Where does Barney live?" Sophie wanted to know.

"I don't think you've seen his little cabin yet...out on the west quarter of the property? That's where Barney stays, though there's a nice apartment over a portion of the barn that he can use, as well. He says he wants to be out surrounded by nature, so the cabin has by far been his favorite place. He doesn't have any close family, and I think he feels at home here."

Barney's arrival at the farm had been unusual, but the children could sense how thankful Aunt Jenny was that he had come to stay. Thinking it all over, Tim made a note to question him about wild animals he'd seen out by the cabin, and then Sophie thought to ask, "How old is Barney?"

"Well, let's see…he was only nineteen when he ran through the fence, so he'd be twenty-four now. I assumed he'd find a girl and have a family someday, but that hasn't happened yet."

They drove the wagon through the entrance with the swinging sign high above, and after Tim pulled the gate shut, he asked, "Hey, can we tell Barney about the bridge and the coins?"

Aunt Jenny suggested they might wait till there was time to tell the whole tale when they were all together. So, the three made a pact to keep their secret and not tell Barney any of the story until Aunt Jenny gave them the signal.

CHAPTER NINETEEN

Barney's Return

The old wagon was just making its turn into the drive by the house when a figure ambled out of the nearest barn. The children waved right away sure that the tall, thin man was Barney.

As they climbed down from the wagon, Aunt Jenny called, "Hallo! Good to have you back and I'd like you to meet Tim and Sophie. Children, this is Barney."

The slender man came over, reached his fingers through the bridle and stroked Donny's head as he grinned a hello at them. "How do you like Misty Glen Farm?"

"We've had the best time and Aunt Jenny is great fun," declared Tim and Sophie together.

"Aunt Jenny, is it? Then you've really felt comfortable here!" Barney teased.

"Well, after I've unhitched this wagon, I'm off to do the rest of the chores. Things sure pile up when one goes away. It was real good to meet you." And with a sincerity of feeling, he shook first Tim's hand and then Sophie's, then led the horse toward the barn.

As they turned to walk up the porch steps, the phone began ringing in the kitchen.

They hurried into the house and Aunt Jenny made a grab for it. Instantly, Tim and Sophie knew she was talking with Dale Lane.

"I watched your activity in town," said the sheriff, "and at the diner. I even trailed you quite a way as you left town. I didn't see anyone suspicious looking or any sign that you were being followed.

"I did ask around to see if anyone had noticed any strangers hanging about or anything else out of the ordinary. Klassen said he hadn't sold anything to any strangers, yet he had been missing some shirts, a pair of jeans, and he couldn't find the new large rope he'd set out the day before. So, I gave him a description of the suspect.

'You bet I'll be watchin',' the storekeeper told me."

Then Dale cautioned Aunt Jenny, "Obviously, my men have been alerted, but do keep your eyes open. Let me know if you see anything and try to keep the children close."

Mrs. MacNeil agreed and the sheriff finished, "I plan to have a couple of deputies stake out the area around the bridge where Tim mapped out his find, and further northeast by the abandoned logging camp. If the guy has traveled that far, he might use one of those old buildings for his hideaway."

"Thanks, Dale," said Aunt Jenny, "I'll try to keep Tam inside as much as possible, too." Then she remembered to tell the sheriff that Barney was back.

CHAPTER TWENTY

Snow Day

Keeping Tam inside proved easier than she expected when the snow began the next morning. It wasn't a soft feathery snow, either, but a wind-blown, biting snow. It looked more like tiny crystals of salt streaking along sideways.

Nevertheless, the snow continued to pile up until it was two feet deep. Esmerelda was escorted into the barn, Donny was kept in his warm stall, and the chickens did not venture a feather from their pen, as neither man nor beast could enjoy being out in that kind of weather.

In the house, the massive stone hearth became the favorite gathering place. Circled round the blazing fire, the children finished books they had brought with them, as well as several great volumes that they found on Aunt Jenny's shelves in a comfortable reading spree that lasted till almost dinnertime.

Around four-thirty the phone began to ring. "I'll just get that," called Aunt Jenny as she moved toward the kitchen and picked up the receiver.

"Jenny, this is Dale. Could you and the children come back to town for a meeting at Sam's, at eight in the morning? I know that's early, but I have a full schedule. Still, I'd like to fill you in on what's been happening."

"We'll be there," said Aunt Jenny, and she put the phone back down. "Well," she said as she entered the living room, "it's back to Hollis tomorrow morning for a meeting with Dale at Mr. Bern's house."

"Does he know something?" asked Tim.

"He didn't tell me," promised Aunt Jenny. "He said he'd fill us all in when he sees us in the morning. We'll have to get going early to be at Mr. Bern's by eight o'clock."

"Oh, that doesn't matter," Sophie assured her. "We can't wait to find out what he wants to tell us!"

"Well, that goes for me, too, but right now I need to start thinking about getting tonight's supper in the oven, and then I'll be gone for a short time while I milk Esmy."

"If you'd like, I'd love to help you with dinner," Sophie said, "and when you put on your coat and boots, I'll start some hot tea for your return!"

CHAPTER TWENTY-ONE

Monopoly and Old Faithful

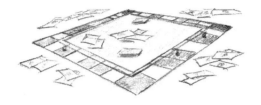

Later, as the clock struck seven, Barney knocked at the door. "Hey, y'all. The chores are finished and I've cleared your walk. Is there anything else you need?"

"Barney," yelled the kids, "come in and play some games with us." So Barney was added to the group that played Monopoly into the evening.

They did stop for supper. After they had passed the platter of meatloaf, bowls of mashed potatoes and Aunt Jenny's special green beans, and after the bread and the butter and the jam had gone round, and just as the chunky applesauce had made its way past everyone, Aunt Jenny winked at the children and asked Barney about his trip.

"Did you have good roads and did you accomplish all you set out to do?"

"Well," Barney began, "the roads were clear, and thankfully I got back before this morning's big snow. There was one incident with a car and truck in front of me that was sort of exciting…at least for a moment, but nothing happened."

He continued, "While I was in Illinois, I did have plenty of time to visit my friends and to see about that new tractor we talked about."

"How did you like it?"

"It was all right, but if we wait another year we could buy one with a lot more options. I can hold 'Old Faithful' together for one more season. What do you think?"

Aunt Jenny considered this for a moment and said, smiling, "I trust you completely. It sounds wise. Hold away!"

Meanwhile, Jenny could tell that the children were bursting to tell their news and finally opened the topic. "Barney, we've had a bit of excitement ourselves...Tim, Sophie?"

And in a great flood of words, Barney learned, as he slowly munched on squares of thick shortbread and drank his tea, all that had been happening while he was away.

First, Tim told about their afternoon hike and how they returned to the railroad bridge the next day. Sophie followed, sharing the whole story of their fall down the creek bank and how Aunt Jenny and Tam had rescued them. Tim finished with all the details of their trip to town and the man at the window.

Barney listened carefully to their stories and whistled low, "Wow! Y'all did have an exciting time!" Then, casting an admiring glance at Mrs. McNeil, he said, "It sounds like you handled that situation and your rope like an expert...a real pro! All that happened on my time off?"

They assured him that it had, and then Aunt Jenny explained that she and the children were returning to town the next day to talk with Dale Lane.

When she finished, Tim and Sophie did not miss the significant glance that passed between Barney and Aunt Jenny. It led them to believe that Barney was planning on keeping a careful watch on the property and especially over the farmhouse.

CHAPTER TWENTY-TWO

Hollis Town Re-Run

Early in the morning, the children found themselves bundling up for another wagon ride to town, or so they thought.

All of a sudden, Barney seemed to appear out of nowhere. It was then the children discovered that Barney had spent the night at his apartment in the barn loft, just to stay close. Their assumption the night before, that he would be watching, had proved correct.

However, when the children turned toward the barn, expecting to see Barney preparing their ride, he wasn't hitching Donny to a wagon at all—he was fitting the big horse up to a sleigh! With the snow they'd received, a sleigh was just the thing. Tim and Sophie were delighted.

As they glided smoothly toward town, bells jingling faintly on the breeze, Tim and Sophie burrowed way down into the blankets, wondering what the sheriff had in mind.

Today, the children didn't look out at as many things as they had on the previous trip to town, for the wind had picked up, making it colder, and they were covered over the top with blankets. Even Aunt Jenny left the horse to follow the road on his own, though she did still have hold of the reins as she snuggled deep into the warmth, right along with the children.

To anyone passing by, it would have appeared as if this sleigh was missing its driver! However, for a driverless sleigh, a great deal of noise issued from the depths of the blankets, including lively muffled talk and now and then a shriek of laughter which just proved that cold or not, these three could always have a good time.

When the group was finally gathered in Mr. Bern's office, Dale pulled two pictures out of a large envelope and passed them around. Tim and Sophie looked at the photographs. "That's him!" they said. Aunt Jenny nodded her head. Yes, this was the man who had come to her door.

"Well, that's interesting," remarked Dale. "About a week ago, there was a robbery. A man in Chicago took a large old trunk into a shop to be repaired. Apparently the owner of the shop found bags of coins carefully hidden in the curved top of the giant trunk's lid. He rather unwisely made a show of his find in front of some patrons at the store whom he did not know. Later that night, and before he could contact the owner of the trunk, the shop was broken into and the coins were found missing.

"The brunt of the investigation so far has been to notify all possible coin collectors, shops, and the like, to watch out for any large sales of coins since they may be stolen. So much time has to be taken up with these efforts that finding the individual responsible has been sort of secondary.

"When I put in a bulletin about a satchel of Dutch coins and a stranger being seen around Hollis, the Chicago authorities requested descriptions. Using all the excellent details that each of you provided, they were able to do a composite, and pull up these pictures from their record files."

Noticing Sophie's puzzled expression, Dale said, "A composite is an attempt to combine together the descriptions of a suspect. Then an artist tries to draw a face that matches all the descriptive clues. With a good composite drawing, it's sometimes possible to search past photo files and find a similar looking face.

"Until your report, there wasn't much evidence about the person who committed the robbery. With your description, these photos were retrieved from the state's main files and this man has become the chief suspect in the case. Apparently, he has prior police records including grand theft, and goes under many an alias."

"Wow," said Tim and Sophie, facing each other, amazed as they remembered their encounter with the man at the bridge, while Aunt Jenny was recalling the shadow at the window, and the man who had threatened her at her very own door!

As Dale continued to speak, they turned back to look at him. "Now, with your positive identification wired to the Chicago police, they can begin to collect evidence on this particular man's activities to verify a trail that will connect him with the actual robbery.

"Meanwhile, we're watching the area where we think he is staying and we are planning to arrest him when we are confident we can do it with all the coins in his possession.

"It's our guess based on the police review that he has several more bags stashed at his hideout. We believe that in his hurry to get away, he somehow lost one bag over the creek bank, realized it later, and went looking for it. He was probably working on a way to recover the bag when you children surprised him. He thought he could just scare you all off. He tried a couple of times, but he didn't know any of you very well, did he?" Dale smiled.

"Now that we know who this man actually is, things should move rapidly.

"Well, we'd best wrap up this meeting. Any questions?"

Tim reached in his pocket for his coin and put it in the hand of the sheriff. Mr. Bern followed suit and gave back the one he had, as well. Then Sophie searched the corner of her jeans pocket and found the one she had carried since that day at the bridge. She gazed at it wistfully before handing it over.

"We sure never thought that we'd find authentic old treasure and hold it in our hands or get to keep it, even for a little while!"

Then Sophie grinned, "What stories we can tell about this holiday vacation!"

Tim laughed and Aunt Jenny turned to her friend, "Thank you Dale, for everything you've done.

"And Mr. Bern, thank you for your time. You were so helpful, encouraging us that what we had was worth finding out about."

CHAPTER TWENTY-THREE

Case Closed

Several days later, the children were deciding what they wanted to do before their vacation ended. This particular cold and blustery morning had turned out perfect for a Scrabble tournament. Even Aunt Jenny had been drawn into the play and three rounds were already completed.

They had stopped for Sophie to make hot cocoa, and she was just reaching for the tall chocolate pot and cups when she glanced out the kitchen window in time to see the sheriff's car pull up and stop in front of the house.

After carefully setting down the pot, Sophie ran to let him in at the door. "Aunt Jenny, Tim, Mr. Lane is here!" When Jenny and Tim joined them, Dale began to relate the events of the night before.

"The patrols we had watching the suspect reported they had witnessed the man recover the green bag at the edge of the creek, and then shadowed him."

Dale grinned, "Apparently my men just let him go after the coins by himself. I guess he had a rather difficult time, with all that new snow. "

Tim and Sophie shook their heads, remembering their fall and imagining how hard it must have been to get down that rocky slope, not to mention trying to find the bag amidst the snowdrifts!

Dale continued, "My men also stated that they followed the suspect to one of the old cabins at the abandoned logging camp.

"We positioned our officers around the area and closed in. We were able to take him by surprise and apprehend the man inside his cabin."

"And the coins?" said Tim.

"According to the report, as best they can determine, all the coins the shopkeeper found in the old trunk were recovered and accounted for," said Dale. "The Chicago authorities have taken over.

"We'll transport the prisoner tomorrow morning. As far as my department is concerned, the case is wrapped up."

"Congratulations Dale! That was good work," said Aunt

Jenny, and they shook hands all around. Sheriff Lane had to leave and they walked him to the door, everyone saying good-bye and thanking him over and over again.

Seeing the sheriff drive away, everyone's first reaction was to let out a big sigh of relief. "Well," said Aunt Jenny, "it's certainly good that the owner recovered his possessions, and that they have the thief in custody. We don't have to worry about him sneaking around anymore." The children agreed.

However, a little later they were somewhat surprised to discover that each of them was also experiencing an empty sort of feeling.

"After all that excitement," said Tim.

"It's just over," Sophie remarked.

"Just like that!" echoed Aunt Jenny. "Case closed!"

Shaking themselves a bit, they returned to their game, but it was funny how many oddly pertinent words popped up on that Scrabble board, words like clue, sheriff, scare, coins, alias, arrest, and robbery. It was easy to see that, case closed or not, the events of the past few days were still very much on their minds.

CHAPTER TWENTY-FOUR

Jenny's Victory

Just before supper, the children began to gather their things from the sitting room and make sure they had all their clothes collected for the packing they would do the next day.

Every now and then Sophie would wander into Tim's bedroom and sit on the bed. She'd start talking about when they learned to feed the chickens, or the first day they met Tam, or the exhilaration of a real sleigh ride; then she would wander out again.

As Tim finished his own chores, he, too, thought over many of the events of the past two weeks. Pondering the day of their rescue, he found his journal in the sitting room and picked up his pen. Under the survival skills section he made a new entry: "When exploring, leave accurate details of your destination." He paused for a moment and then added, "And then for your own safety, be where you said you'd be!"

Just as he was closing his journal, he heard Aunt Jenny calling, "Supper's on!" and he joined his sister as they walked down the familiar winding staircase to the dining room.

Much later, they spent their evening with Aunt Jenny enjoying bowls of popcorn, pieces of sweet apple, and a great chapter book that Jenny had begun reading to them several days ago. The fire slowly hissed and sputtered on the hearth in a sing-songy sort of way and sleepy heads began to bob. Marking the chapter and gently closing the book, Aunt Jenny smiled at the children. "Because you look ready for bed and since I could never get you up there by myself, it's probably time to say goodnight.

"I think we can finish this book tomorrow after lunch," Aunt Jenny added for the benefit of Sophie, who was still looking behind her as if she expected more of the story, even as she climbed each stair.

Aunt Jenny, watching them go to bed, smiled a rather plaintive smile. "Enough of that!" she chastened herself. "Rejoice in the fun times ye've had and dinna ye be goin' all maudlin!"

As was her habit, she lapsed into the brogue of her ancestors when tired or a bit melancholy.

But, catching herself, she said, "Look forward, not back," and the sorrow left her as she happily gave herself to planning the last full day that the children would spend at Misty Glen Farm.

First they would go to their little white church at River Bend, and in addition she thought a winter picnic might be just the thing to brighten all their spirits!

CHAPTER TWENTY-FIVE

Sunday Sleigh Ride

Sunday morning dawned clear, temperature in the thirties, and the sleigh ride to church looked exactly like an old winter postcard. A thin layer of snow had fallen in addition to the big snow of several days ago. Everything looked fresh and sparkling white. The sleigh barely held all of them, Aunt Jenny, Barney, Sophie, and Tim. But, the closeness kept them good and warm as they skimmed along the old belt road that seldom saw a plow.

Deep in the blankets Tim and Sophie were happily recalling their breakfast. Barney had been invited and there had been heaps of pancakes, light and tender in the center, crispy on the edges; fat, well-browned sausages; fresh butter and milk from Esmy; along with a tall green pitcher of real maple syrup.

As he fixed his pancakes, Barney said, "Did you know this syrup was made from the maple trees right here at Misty Glen?"

"Where are the maples?" asked Tim.

Aunt Jenny looked up from flipping more pancakes and replied, "You know the trees lining our long drive...the tall ones you see when you first get here? Those are our oldest maples and then there are smaller groves of them all over the property."

Barney continued, "We tap the trees and send the sap down the road. There's a family close to Hollis that's been making maple syrup for generations. We sell most of our sap to them, but we barter a bit of it and for that we get a few jugs full of finished maple syrup!"

As Barney was explaining the process, both he and Aunt Jenny were thoroughly amused at the number of pancakes Tim and Sophie were consuming. When the children could not eat another bite, the older two broke into a teasing applause and they all laughed together.

Then they chattered away as they washed the dishes, but before anyone put on his coat, everyone drank a last cup of hot tea, "for the warmin'" as Aunt Jenny declared. Now they were flying through the countryside on their way to Sunday service and only their noses were feeling any cold.

When the cozy riders reached the church and had secured the sleigh, they were all greeted with enthusiastic hugs and hearty handshakes. Neighbors and townspeople were all glad to see Aunt Jenny and Barney, and grateful to catch up on news. Making their way to the special young visitors they welcomed them, as well.

After the ringing of the steeple bell faded away, the organ music began to draw everyone out of the cold and right into the church building. From the white wood and stone pulpit draped in pale green cloth, the pastor spoke about making and keeping friends, a message which seemed perfectly appropriate to the children who felt like Barney and Aunt Jenny had become wonderful friends—ones they definitely wanted to keep.

Sophie and Tim especially loved the story of David and Jonathan and the genuine friendship of two people who had lived so long ago. After the story was over, everyone stood to sing the hymn "What a Friend We Have in Jesus," then they left the wooden pews and filed out of the church, encouraged for the week, and appreciating the time they had to worship together.

On the drive back to the farm, Aunt Jenny surprised the children with the idea of a winter picnic. "You mean we'll actually sit outside and eat?" said Tim.

"What will we do to keep warm?" asked Sophie, and Barney laughed.

Aunt Jenny said, "Trust me," with a twinkle in her eye, and that was all she would say.

CHAPTER TWENTY-SIX

Winter Picnic

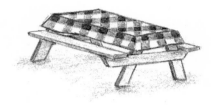

As soon as they returned to the farm, Aunt Jenny instructed Tim and Sophie to dress warmly in play clothes and meet her in the kitchen.

"Okay, we're warm as toast and ready to go!" said Sophie as she and Tim rounded the corner and found Aunt Jenny placing items on a large tray. So far, she had hotdogs, a package of soft buns, mustard, and catsup, and she was just adding the pickle relish and a spoon.

"Tim, would you please carry that box?" she asked. "It has a big can of beans, spoons and bowls, and some hot chocolate mix. Oh! Here is a can opener to add, and some cups."

After dropping in the last items, Tim shouldered the carton of food and supplies. Aunt Jenny handed Sophie a red checked tablecloth, and one bag of potato chips and another of marshmallows, saying, "I'll just carry the tray and you can follow me."

Aunt Jenny, warmly dressed in a sweater, jeans, a plaid wool coat, and with a lengthy red muffler wrapped around her neck, carried the tray to the backyard where the fire pit was located.

A heavy stone structure with a high back to cut the wind, this fire pit had a large set-in grate under which the fire was laid and over which things could be placed to cook. "It's our kitchen for the day!" beamed Aunt Jenny.

Barney had started the fire earlier and the coals were almost ready for hot dogs. Sophie spread the cloth over the picnic table which had been swept clear of snow and Aunt Jenny set the tray down, while directing Tim to put the box on the stone shelf to the left side of the fire pit.

"All right, everyone," Aunt Jenny laughed, as she stepped back from the table, "rule number one for winter picnics is that whenever you are cold you come close to the fire and warm up. Rule number two is to play lots of running games, like races and tag, which, I have to admit, is usually quite funny in the snow."

As it turned out, however, besides roasting sizzling hot-dogs on long sticks, eating the beans which had bubbled hot in the can on the grate, and one long hysterical game of tag in which there was much laughing and falling down, the main activity turned out to be two snow forts and an afternoon snowball fight—Barney and Tim against Aunt Jenny and Sophie.

"Hey, here's one for you!" yelled Tim as he lobbed a snow-ball across the yard.

"And back at you," Sophie screeched, as with surprising aim she and Aunt Jenny fired a salvo of balls toward the men. Tam kept busy racing after all the snowy missiles, leaping and barking, though he rarely caught one himself.

Somehow, with all the activity, no one remembered it was cold, though later they drew close around the fire to which wood had been added. Here they toasted their marshmallows to a deep golden brown, drank rich cocoa, and listened while Aunt Jenny read. True to her word, Aunt Jenny finished the book she had been reading to the children the night before, and at the ending Sophie sighed a deep sigh.

"This was a perfect day," she murmured, "A perfect last day for a winter picnic."

CHAPTER TWENTY-SEVEN

Good-bye Plans

Dad was on his way to pick them up, and they were ready. Tim and Sophie, remembering their first trip to town, thought about the day they had eaten lunch at the diner and bought the gifts for Kip and Sara. Those presents had been wrapped and carefully packed away in their soft-sided suitcases and Tim and Sophie were savoring their last hours on the farm.

Early that morning they'd taken Donny out for a long ride. Having learned to sit doubled-up bareback to stay warm, they had ridden along, trying to memorize their favorite sights: the steep drops of the sandy cliffs, how the winter light fell across the hills, and the shimmering snow over the frozen pond.

Now they were saying their good-byes to the gentle old horse. As he lowered his head toward her, Sophie hugged the huge face tightly and bestowed many kisses on his gigantic soft nose, imploring him not to forget her.

Tim gave his special attention to Tam, who had devotedly followed him everywhere since the day of their rescue at the bridge. The dog licked Tim's hand and Tim buried it deeply in the silky fur, giving Tam's neck a hearty love-filled scruffing.

Yet, what the children dreaded the most was saying good-bye to Aunt Jenny. Such a kind, warm-hearted woman, she had proved to be a genuine treasure, and Tim and Sophie loved her dearly.

As she placed cold fried chicken and potato salad out for their lunch, Aunt Jenny said, "I hope you've enjoyed visiting here as much as I've loved every minute having you."

"Oh, yes!" Tim and Sophie shouted out in unison.

"Well," she suggested, "you might be thinking of what you'd like to do this summer."

"What?" Both children's heads popped up and they looked straight into her eyes, "Could we come back?"

"We really want to!"

"May we?"

Afterward they gathered close together and talked about possible times and dates, contingent of course on their parents' permission, and the children assured Aunt Jenny that they would write often.

"We want to stay in touch with you...and Barney," piped Sophie.

Her brother nodded and grinned, "We want to keep up with all the news here."

Reward

The children returned home, resumed their schooling, and thought often of Aunt Jenny and all the events of their time at the farm. Several months later a large envelope arrived by courier.

It was addressed to Tim and Sophie Bigelow, and their father handed it to them, watching to see what it contained. As Tim opened the envelope, he found inside a letter, and two cases, each with a coin. "Hey," said Sophie, "those are some of the coins we found on the farm!"

The letter read:

Dear Tim and Sophie Bigelow,

I would be gravely negligent not to thank the children who were so instrumental in helping solve the case of the missing coins, though I didn't know I had missing coins until after the robbery. Apparently these coins belonged to my great-uncle and to his father before him, and were already years old when they first came into our family.

They are precious to me, not only for the monetary value and for the fact that they have history, but also for family sentiment.

When I heard what had happened, I was sorry that they had been lost, and I rejoiced when they were found.

I'm enclosing a check for a reward. Perhaps this money can go a bit toward a college fund for the two brave detectives that helped return the treasure.

As an additional portion of the reward, I wish to share one of these special coins with each of you as I heard how you returned all of them immediately when you found the real owner. Perhaps they will entice you to begin a collection of your own.

Someday, I may be able to meet you both and say in person how much I appreciate all that you did.

With gratitude,
Garrit Harlingen